PJMASKS
Christmas Wishes

eOne™   FROG BOX

SIMON SPOTLIGHT • An imprint of Simon & Schuster Children's Publishing Division • New York   London   Toronto   Sydney   New Delhi • 1230 Avenue of the Americas, New York, New York 10020
This Simon Spotlight edition September 2018 • This book is based on the TV series PJ MASKS © Frog Box / Entertainment One UK Limited / Walt Disney EMEA Productions Limited 2014.
Les Pyjamasques by Romuald © (2007) Gallimard Jeunesse. All Rights Reserved. This book/publication © Entertainment One UK Limited 2018. Adapted by Maggie Testa from the series
PJ Masks. All rights reserved, including the right of reproduction in whole or in part in any form. SIMON SPOTLIGHT and colophon are registered trademarks of Simon & Schuster, Inc.
For information about special discounts for bulk purchases, please contact Simon & Schuster Special Sales at 1-866-506-1949 or business@simonandschuster.com. Manufactured in China 0718 RKT
2 4 6 8 10 9 7 5 3 1 ISBN 978-1-5344-2059-5 ISBN 978-1-5344-2060-1 (eBook)

It's the right time for Christmastime, and the PJ Masks can't wait. There are presents to give and presents to receive, but the PJ Masks know that Christmas is about so much more than that.

"What is your Christmas wish, Catboy?" asks Gekko.

"Well, I already have the best friends anyone could ever ask for," says Catboy.

"So my Christmas wish is to make new friends, like the time we made friends with a teeny-weeny Ninjalino! Making new friends is the cat's whiskers!"

"What is your Christmas wish, Owlette?" asks Catboy.

"I wish for everyone to be kind to one another on Christmas and every day of the year . . .

". . . like the time we went ice-skating with Luna Girl. We might not always get along with Luna Girl, but that night we had a lot of fun being together."

Gekko thinks about all the great things that will happen in the coming year.

"My wish is to grow bigger and stronger every day . . .

"...but I know that my Super Gekko Muscles are strongest when we work together."

Suddenly Catboy notices that the PJ Masks have company. "Look! It's Night Ninja, Luna Girl, and Romeo!" he says.

"What are you up to?" asks Owlette.

"We heard your Christmas wishes, and we'd like to tell you ours," says Night Ninja.

"'Tis the season for Christmas music," Night Ninja continues. "My Christmas wish is for me and my Ninjalinos to take our act on the road."

"My moths and I will come with you!" says Luna Girl.

"My Christmas wish is that everyone gets what they wish for . . . especially me!" Luna Girl loves Christmas.

"Being together with my best friend is my Christmas wish," says Romeo, thinking about his robot.

"And I have a Christmas gift for you, PJ Masks. I promise not to take over the world . . . until next year!"

What will you wish for this Christmas? Merry Christmas to little heroes everywhere!